MALEFICENT MORTALS

Published By

MALEFICENT MORTALS

Compiled and Edited by

Sujata Nayak

EDITOR'S BIO

She is a Bungler ink slinger. She pens out the ardour that drips from her fingertips.

Avocation – Dance, Artist, crafts, sporty fellow, explorer, photography. Introvert but bleeds on paper. She has been involved in few endeavours of literary world. She is a Laconic & an Acosmist. She strives to share her vision with readers & inspire them to explore themselves.

Instagram handle- @suju_nayak

@vagabonding_encephalon

EDITOR'S NOTE

Above all to the Almighty God, for the psychic enlightenment, the insight and unending flow of ideas which help a potent deal; for lighting up the lantern of wish, encouragement, spirit and serenity to the success of this book to finish.

I pay my deep sense of gratitude to my caring and loving support system Late Satyabadi Nayak and Late Sanjukta Nayak for their elevating inspiration. Being the example of virtuous humans who served the environment with their kindness and beautiful mind, they ignited the spark in me to compile "MALEFICIENT MORTALS".

Thanks to all the authors who have shared their efforts and support to make this endeavour a reality.

Last, but not the least, "MY READERS" are important inspiration for me. Thanks for the love and support. This one's for you.

CONTENTS

————◦❧◦————

INHUMAN HUMAN

Sujata Nayak

"Earth doesn't belong to us, we belong to earth. This earth was made for all beings not just Human Beings. The earth is large enough to share but mankind's heart is not large enough to care. Saving wildlife is the first step towards saving the environment. The earth looks more beautiful with animals rather than Human Beings. Giver of happiness always get joys and love rather than taker of happiness. The extent of cruelty that the humans are spreading these days is unbearable and one could be heartbroken with the same. The world environment day just passed away few months ago. The crime towards the nature and especially towards the lives of others committed by humanity are so odious, its better not to even utter about the incident that what happened and how.

Such an incident happened in 27 May 2020 in Kerala in which both mother and baby elephant got killed by the villagers. It's hard to understand that how the essence of humanity could escape someone to this extent that they allowed themselves to do such an inhumane activity. She was pregnant and hungry. And the villagers fed her with a pineapple stuffed with crackers. The only mistake that the mother elephant did that she believed 'INHUMAN HUMANS'. Truth be told, the current times really can be characterized as "the rage of inhumanity." It's not only the loss to biodiversity but also a severe loss to the on-going life cycle.

Nature everywhere is declining at a speed never previously seen and our need for ever more food and energy are the main drivers. From the bees that pollinate our crops, to the forests that hold back flood waters, the humans are ravaging the very ecosystems that support their societies.

Protecting plants and animals will lead the way in protecting and saving the humanity. No matter how many money we have, loving wildlife and nature will make us rich beyond measure. Don't treat animals as animals. Treat them as living beings that's what they are.

"SAVE ENVIRONMENT SAVE LIFE."

EVILS IN HUMAN NATURE

Gousia Ajaz Khan

Evil is poisoning and disposing the pearl of politeness and
goodness, have we humans lost the feeling of care and
consciousness?
Is our vicious nature revealing itself and making it more
obvious and ridiculous.
Making the poor work as machines, tirelessly labouring as the
inanimate entities.
Why can't we think of the consequences, dehumanizing them
would lead to more evilness and cruelty?
Conversely animals are overridden across the streets and left
unattended and overlooked.
Indulging and forcing women and children into the hell of
prostitution and exploitation.
Depriving the backwards and minorities of their rights,
pushing the young youth into the malicious activities.
We people have become ruthlessly so insolent, filming other
people's tragedies and unfortunate events
is in vogue.
Before we completely twirl the world into shelter of beasts
think over before you do something evil
and villainous.

RAGING IMMORTALITY
Saumya Chauhan

I was walking home with my 2 friends, after college farewell. We took bus from college to home. We three were childhood friends. Ritika and Rashmi were cousins and lived under same roof, right next to me. There were 4 man grouped near a bike. We 3 were, talking and giggling. It got their unwanted attention. One of those four, said in a teasing way..."Oho, what is so funny madam, tell us too. And they laughed hard.

We ignored, and kept walking. Rashmi wanted to stop and give him a nice beating. She was a karate black belt. But I stopped her. I didn't want us to get in any trouble. Ritika was very sensitive girl since childhood. She was scared and was rushing in order to reach home fast. Another one again spoke, "we are all alone in this world, we can use your company, come here, let's have fun".

I was angry. And wanted to give them the answer they deserved, but no. I am actually very calm person. But that day, I sensed a rage building up inside me slowly. May be it was all the collection of emotions, which I ignored all the way from beginning, to keep myself calm. Suddenly my heels broke. Enjoying all this, the third man came a little closer to us, grabbed me, with an evil smirk on face, he said "my queen, let me give you a good ride".

The moment this happened, I felt rage gushing in my veins. As if I am going to burst with anger. I looked at him, my eyes were red. He got scared, and stepped back. I walked towards him, and gave him a hard slap. He fell on ground, groaning in pain. I saw another coming and I don't know from where, I felt a sudden power emerging inside me. My face was all red with bloody eyes. I was in yellow Saree and fire surrounding my body. But it couldn't hurt me, as my rage was fuelling the fire. My hair was all messed and I turned into a powerful humanly animal. The moon witnessing all this turned red. The wind was howling.

I forced man on the ground so hard that he died. But my rage couldn't stop. A supernatural power resided inside me. As if it was serving its purpose but wanted more.

Shikha stop! Rashmi screamed with pain and fear in her eyes. Her voice had care for me. I suddenly opened my eyes, to heavy knock on my room's door. Rashmi and Ritika entered the room with bags and said, "girl, why are you still in bed? We have class in one hour. "I smiled and sighed with relief, that it was a nightmare.

Sometimes, it's important to express your emotions. One should know how to control them too. Be it any emotion. Too much of anything, will end up hurting you and your loved ones. Too much controlled emotions can make you a raging malefic beast.

A DEAL WITH EVIL

Venkat Singh

We the humans are not so good,

Many of us never took a side and stood,

We have done a lot of damage to the society,

We are doing worst and showing our cruelty,

We exploit the nature to our benefits,

We never give the nature coz that

giving things never fits,

We not only use animals for our use,

We show our evilness by exploiting the poor

for creating goods,

We can do anything for our benefits and our own good sake,

Coz we are in the skin of humans with the nature of snake,

We hurt the emotions of the one, who shows it,

We don't care and ignore them like shit,

We are the ones, who created the

words like depression,

We are the reason for the detachment with good deeds and

separation,

We are like the hawk,

Who can trade the dead for

own beneficial walk,

We are the one, who is responsible

for the dirty politics,

It's not their fault coz we are responsible
for this bad shit.
We are those so called literate,
Who can drag our own people to hell crate?
But still,
It's not like we all are bad.
The trend of being good is just fade.
Many of us take a stand,
And make the society good
by their working hands.
Many of us have been a nature lover,
We planted trees and give them a cover.
Some of us also show care
and are priest hearted,
Coz we can't take the things for granted.
Many of them are God's angel to society by
keeping humanity.
All hearts are not filled with evilness n cruelty.
Because where there is evil
there also lives a God.
Who makes the society the mother earth a great
place for all.

SHE ISN'T WEAK!

Shreya Gardas

"She isn't weak"

"She"....got raped when she wore a Saree, when she wore a
skirt, when she is 6, when she is 60; actually "she got raped"
isn't right!

He raped her! Is the reality?

These men respect their mother, care their sister, and love
their wife.

But their evilness spoils someone's daughter, kill someone's
happiness, hurt someone's body.

She's never afraid of horror stories coz her mind is already
flooded with series of restrictions, judgements, conditions
gifted by society.

But listen!

She isn't weak to get dominated.

She can handle her career and her family.

She can't be forced to wear bindi or bangles it's her wish to be.

She can wear shorts or skirts it's her comfort. You can't judge
her.

She can be independent and confident.

She is strong and she can scream louder when injustice comes
her way and all she deserves is...

Safety, Respect,

Happiness, Freedom.

'She isn't weak"

EVIL BY CHOICE

Ananya Barik

No human is born evil.

The way he moulds his cerebration

makes him evil.

Detachment from the loved ones

frames him to evil.

Lack of morals turns him to evil.

Fear of getting lost in the big stage

bring forth evil.

The way he absorbs other's opinions shapes him to evil.

And this evil leads to deaths, conflicts, accidents and hatred

among people.

The world should be reminded

Of the good deeds,

Of temperance,

Of magnificence,

Of patience,

Of truthfulness,

Of ambition,

Of friendliness,

Of magnanimity,

As virtue is the path to contentment.

IMMORAL BEHAVIOUR

Dishaben Patel

As you grow older and think that you have seen everything or almost everything, life will come to refute you by sending you experiences and lessons that and these will be the basic raw material of your emotional adulthood.

Each of us has experienced in different ways and in various forms manifestations of jealousy and malice. Maybe you, like most people are trying to find the cause the reason for an unwarranted backstabbing knife, while struggling to heal your wounds at the same time.

But who are these people?

A question we all know but never tried to identify these people! Firstly, those who do not respect the particularities and boundaries of each person and violating it continuously. Secondly, those who do not respect you, your family and the people in your life. Thirdly, all those who have repeatedly shown that they are not happy with your joy, and cannot feel sad with your sadness.

How to deal with evil starting with protecting yourself? Remember that you and only you can control the reaction; you will not have to show that to the malice people. You may not be able to control many of the conditions and many of the events that happen in your life, but with practise you can learn how to react to the negative challenges of people...

How to deal with evil but also the person from whom it arises?

Difficult to answer but they are some clues that totally suits with the question. Starting with, the best solution is to reduce time with them, try if it is possible to get them out of your life completely. Reconcile with the real face of evil, once you have passed the first stage of awareness and pain, face and compromise with the idea of. YES! There is no much evil out there and that is a part of our life too.

To conclude, you believe, you hope, you wish the person to change and you vainly believing that at some points he/she will understand the magnitude of his immoral behaviour. Getting rid of high expectations that will never be confirmed is literally the biggest release.

THE DARK SKY

Jasmine Parveen

Look at the sky, look at the land,

And look at the reason behind it.

The temperature of 50° Celsius,

Thousands of disease.

Look at the number of crime,

Increases every day.

I can see people being good,

But they are so devil inside.

The devil inside us is still alive,

He knows that God is still locked inside.

For sure, goodness will be gone soon,

Humanity will be lost soon.

God is crying, sitting somewhere

over the rainbow,

He can't see the pain of his children so from us, he took off his

shadow.

The battle is not between love and hate,

But it is about rising love over hate.

When the earth will end, is it still a mystery?

But for sure the humanity is ending,

That is the cause of my misery.

THE REALITY WE LIVE IN

Vaishali. L. S

The noises from the background faded away as I took a deep calming breath. I kept on repeating to myself that I can do it. After all this is not the first time I'm facing a bunch of unknown people for an interview. It's been long but I'm good.

The host approached me with a jittery smile plastered on her face, from the looks of it, I was definitely sure this was her first interview and she was putting on a brave face but I didn't want to call her upon it. And then it all started.

"Good morning everyone, as we are starting a new episode of "Warriors in life", here we have with us, a person who is well known to put the spectres back in closet.

"So tell me Dr How did you choose this field?"
That made me smile,

"From my younger age I was very happy helping others, doing them favours and I never expected anything in return. We face many problems but we bury that inside us, this can damage a person's feelings and mentality very differently. All I do is talk to them, words have the power to both heal and harm, I use them to heal my patients."

"That's impressive. So don't mind me asking but was there any real life experience from your past life that made you more effective in your therapy. what I meant is there any hidden skeletons in your closet?" Eva gave me a conflicted look as she finished reading from the tab in which she had questions coming from the writer of the show.

I gave a nod.

"I don't have a shady past though; I lost my daughter nearly 8 years ago. Riya helped a girl from being bullied by her seniors. The girl afterward tried to suicide, because her parents were at a verge of divorce and she was under a lot of pressure. Being a single mother I understood the feelings that poor girl was facing. Riya was constantly pestered by the senior boys at college because she saved the girl. One night when she was returning home, those boys attacked her and she was thrown in front of a car which was coming off balance, she died on spot."

"I'm so very sorry for bringing that up, may her soul rest in peace. Ma'am after hearing this I have a personal question to ask you. May I?

I nodded at her.

"What are the extents of cases that you have dealt with and how traumatized are the people who comes to you?"

"From my personal experience I can say that people are like cats from outside and monsters or vultures from inside. They treat the ones around them as their own property, they don't consider them humans. Some people are traumatized or have psychotic issues in their past which comes out as a carnal behaviour. The issues around us happen when a person loses self-control and jumps upon opportunities that can damage them to a very long extent. When something happens to you, only you are blamed and the culprit is set free. The side effects of keeping things to ourselves are over stress and anxiety which may lead to excessive depression and sometimes suicidal thoughts. So let it all out and lead a beautiful life ahead that's all I have to say, Thank you."

"Thank you so much Dr Satakshi Verma for taking your precious time and talking with us."

FAULT?? BUT WHOSE??

Iqra Solkar

Sunita was a pure soul. Never thought of any sin. Always loving and helping people. The only thing she was afraid of that if she will does something wrong the most loved thing of her will be snatched away. All was going well unless that day arrived which suddenly changed her whole life. While returning home from school she sensed something suspicious in a house, she thought to go and check if someone needs help or what? Her eyes were shocked to see a murder, she got scared unable to think what to do but managed to call police but ended up getting caught by the murderers.

After a great struggle she escapes but they hit her hard on head she started to faint but still runs to get help from surrounding she shouts for help but no one listens and those who listened they bend over she was helpless to see such evilness of people whom she used to help without any repay again they hit her and this time she fell unconscious the dragged her the whole way and went to forest they took advantage of her, she was already mentally and emotionally broken because of rape she broke physically too. Two gunshots and she breathed her last....

All the evidence were tampered two brutal murders one which had so many eyewitnesses but all shut. The human who helped everyone selflessly didn't get a single help is this really humanity or they are evils by humanity?

EVIL HANDS OF MIND

J.Vetri Michael Raj K.

I told you, we don't have to go easy on Fidel. I can understand your situation; your father's debt needs to be cleared. But he's the reason for your father's death. You can't expect charity from him, he won't help you. Even if we take legal action against him he knows to get rid of it, he owns influential lawyers of this city.

Look Corvin I really want to help you, you are my good friend not because you helped me during my stepsister incident. Your father was the founder of the Corvin finance company; Fidel tricked your father, stole all his shares, and finally made him to suicide. Your silence makes me sad Corvin. Maybe I should contact the community fund chairman for some help.

Hey drop me by Next Street; I have to check-in the Hansel home for family services. Take my car, go to your home and take a nap. We'll meet tonight at the cafe.

(Corvin stops the car and Rafael gets out of the car)

And Corvin I promise you, we'll sort out this problem.

(At his home, Corvin lies in his father's sofa)

Without my father, I can only feel the emptiness here. He has been a good father, he wanted me to study in business school, I didn't want to. But he never compelled me to change my ambition for him. He selected his worker Fidel as his partner, he never believed that tycoon turn against him. My father's depression is mostly for him not for his money.

(Corvin smokes his cigarette)

Laura, Rafal's stepsister, her face will never fade from my memory. She was also a caring and religious person. She worked hard for the community. She never thought the chairman had an eye on her. The chairman raped Laura, she garrotted herself of guilt. After his sister's suicide Rafal became broken. I compromised Rafal and the community officials. They agreed to give him the assistant servicemen job and a large sum of money. He is a good man. I settled him to do that.

(Suddenly Corvin checks his father's closet and takes out something, he leaves his home)

"Rafal it's me'

"Corvin where are you?"

"Listen to me carefully; my father and your sister are prey for these evil humans. I want to apologize for making you do the wrong things. I'm worse than the chairman raped Laura. I'm sorry and my father and your sister need judgment. Maybe What I am going to do now is evil, but I don't care"

"Wait, hold on..." (Corvin hangs up)

(Corvin enters into the restaurant, he sees Fidel having dinner with his family, and he goes near him and aims his father's gun to his head and says)

"You deserve this Fidel" (Corvin shoots Fidel in his head)

(After Fidel slumps on the table Fidel looks at his family and says)

"I am sorry"

(He shoots himself).

JOURNEY WITH THE THERAPIST

R.Susanna Celsia

All around me i see Evil and who is to be blamed? Anyone who does Evil or the cause for Evil...

Let me take you deeper now, hold my hand and come along, you see these people so happy carving stones? The smile or their faces and how satisfied they are.

They are the reason for all the Evil around us today, I can see that question mark on your face and that frown of extreme disagreement controlled,

If you still trust me i will continue. So they multiplier and multiplied and did a lot of good i don't deny, but no one knew who set these standards.. Standards that defined success and failure, standards that missed out happiness and purpose, I see you more confused and your brain toasted Hold on, I have more to show you

So these standards can't be fulfilled by anyone, you ask why i say learn from animals they live in a jungle with the best ethics and probably correct each other saying don't behave like a human? Who knows? They don't have a common standard, a monkey jumps and fish swims they understand their uniqueness and never pushed away another i have seen ants that carry wounded ants, I have seen humans who wounded another human to go forward in his track? You feel its so clumsy and messy.

Now listen intently.

Don't look at the mess, look at yourself how beautiful and unique, I know you still look at yourself through the lenses of standards, leave it aside, you are perfect the way God made you walk this beautiful life receiving happiness and fulfilling your unique purpose...

Still hold on and listen

Now can you find room for envy, strife, jealousy, hatred, malice and all the evil roots?

It's still a confusing story isn't it? But clear too.

UNTOUCHABLES

Living Sunflower

Eyes glued on the television

When at rest?

It is on the mobile phone

Watching yet another story

Of the evils by humanity

A golden laiden man

Distributing one grain of rice

Already on the headline

A thousand likes a thousand shares

Fame, that's on time

How about the elephants

The mother and the daughter

Still fresh on its womb

The humanity killed them through a bomb

And I am just a sad lady

I can do nothing for everybody

So I wrote a poem for the humanity

Where evils live including me

Shall my words live, shall my words die

I don't want to belong, in this society.

WISHPERING OF EVILS

Thiruvikram S

We know we all humans,

Everyone here is with a heart,

Sometimes it goes helpless,

We shift as evil and give rise

To some evilness,

Beasts are better than us with

The limited sense,

We're gradually murdering humanity

By asserting that we are humans,

In sometimes wealth and strength

Makes humanity to recede,

Not everyone is here with a good heart

Kindness should be learned

Everyone here to quit the

Enormity among the humans,

Let's do it and live as kind humans.

MASK OF EVIL

Jayashree Sahoo

Humans are real evil and so dumb in nowadays.
They contuse living animals for
their self-desire.
They kill their own humanity in those
darkest fair.
They give restless tormenting which
suits them best.
They drink blood be change of water
for self-own.
They chase down for money by forgetting
own perfection.
They doing so nefarious work for
own satisfaction.
They shatter; they grind those homely animals for
their pleasure.
They are crude, bad, and so much of abysmal by
their behaviour.
Would they save a life which meant loosing something
of importance?
Will they jump for a life as they watch you fall in
a darkest sense?
Just like evil, they are terror in horror
Just like evil, they show bad kinds of fear
In reality, humans are real evil.

CAGE FELT SAFER

Meghana

Caged like a bird,

in my own house.

And the one need to be caged

is ruling the world out.

Felt to escape

From this jail

I realised that the outside world

Is no more a safe place.

Returned in the same way

I took to escape and

Locked myself

Back in the cage.

Because my heart felt

Let the cage be small.

It is at least safer

When compared to the outside hell.

MY DEAR HUMANS

Dixsaya Rani S

Dear Humans,

Do you remember the days, when we lived together in the same home? Though we had to depend on each other for food and living, we lived a happy life and enjoyed the nature in its purest form. Later, you grew too different from us so you made a separate home for you and went away. Now, you are back. You are always welcome. But you didn't come as a guest or as family, you came here to take our home to yourself and shoo us away. Weren't we the same family? Though we can't live together anymore, why can't you leave us to live in peace?

Yours Lovingly,

Animals

EVIL MIND

Kashish Gagrani

All the evils being done by humanity,

Results from intentions and feelings,

intuition and law being killed,

By, virus of ego, small enough,

Fire of jealousy, hot enough,

Storm of anger, uncontrollable,

Drought of Lies and manipulation ,

Colourless False assumptions through judgement,

Which should be overpowered by?

Vaccine that help one to be flexible enough,

Love of humanity, warm enough,

Shelter of kindness firm enough,

Rain of trust, romantic enough,

Rainbow of understanding and empathy

Beautiful enough. This is tough.

So could only be done by persons who are God's

favorite enough.

THE SIN IS TRAPPED

G L Chandana

There was a man who had two children. The girl Shagun was younger than the Sumit who use to beat his sister always. One day Shagun saw Sumit with some other boys while taking drugs. Their parents went there relatives' house for wedlock.

Shagun did with contention to not do those bad things with his friends but unfortunately, Shagun capitulated to his beating though he had not intended to kill her. But when Shagun was dead Sumit became fearful of their parents and relatives. In a state of being anxious, he came out of his house and met his friend to the whole he posed his problem.

The friend told that to invite a young boy to his house and behead him and put the severed head next to his sister's corpse. Then he would tell his parents that he had found them together, on the bed while he reached home by his friends and was unable to control his fury and slew them both.

Sumit liked the idea and sat at the out of the doorway in the forecasting of a youth. After a few minutes, a handsome young boy passed by the way. He invited him by saying that his sister is not well and needs help to take her to the hospital. The young boy trusted him and went inside to help but Sumit headed him. Then he calls for the parents & relatives and told them the fictitious story.

By seeing everything they were satisfied with him. But the friend who had devised this plan had two cousins who came for vacation and one of them did not reach home that day. Their family was in tension by searching for his cousin. Later the friend came to the house of the Sumit and asked whether he had offered evil advice and asked him that he carried out the plan suggested by him. Yes, of course, it was done successfully said...Sumit took his friend near the dead bodies. He was shocked when he saw that the young boy he had killed was his own cousin. His evil advice caused the death of his own innocent cousin and their own family.

We all do mistakes but when the mistakes went evil it returns to us and according to the Holy books they are many sayings about the evil done by our humans and human.

DEATH OF HUMANITY

Kunalkumar sunesara

In normal terms we can often see in newspaper India is growing in tremendous way. But in actual things are different. There are several aspects other than GDP growth that shows that country is not on right track.

It was late night. Few men following a girl named Shikha. She was on a path of home. It was a 11'o clock at dark night. She usually get late due to her company policy. She was a jubilant girl.

First she ignored them. They kept following her and said bad words and started misbehaving with her.

She ignored. May be it was her mistake.

She reached her home. Next day she was on same time and same place going home. Same group of people try to harass her this time they had higher intensity. They try to touch her and try to grab her but again she made a mistake by not telling anyone. And she reached home anyhow. After reaching home she cried a lot while washing her hand and the glimpses kept coming in her mind of those incidents. She remember when she was a child same incident happened.

With her when her uncle try to give her chocolate and touching her in bad way. This night is full of up and down.

Anyhow she tried to sleep. Next day she got ready with new hope and joy.

But she had no idea what was going to happen today. After completing her work, she was going to home. A group of people try to capture her this time. One person try to rape her and torn off her clothes. 3 men raped her one by one. After rape they kill her and throw her

body in a river. Her family, friends has no idea where is she? They filed an FIR for missing report. They found her body from river after 48 hours. Her face was changed completely. She is no more in this insane world. When police try to investigate it took 3 year for justice.

Many people talks she made wrong choice by going to late night company But no one is safe. It's our responsibility to provide security and change the mind-set.

When police investigate case co-worker of company did not co-operate. All have wrong mind-set. Those bunch of culprit people because India is growing in trade but not mind-set wise.

HAUNTED NIGHT

Diya Jain

Amidst the melancholy darkness of the moonless night,

She got devoured by the dark haunted sight,

Where the bats screech and heavenly

bodies float,

She rambled scared to death on the abandoned road.

Mummies from mausoleum stalked the street,

Her mouth got zipped and anxiousness

froze her feet.

She murmured and silently forged ahead,

Accidently stepped on a dead black cat head.

Her carcass shivered as if froze to death,

As blood commenced rolling sprightly

down her neck.

A shadow appeared and faded away,

Shriek, screams and spooky laughers accompanied

her way.

Eerie sounds flooded the air,

Soaking the innocent in deep despair.

A woman in white invaded her way,

Flitting with a blood stained knife with sway.

She attempted to escape her wizardry eyes,

But was caught and promised a vicious demise.

Fortunately was she rescued from

this ghostly dare?

As she stepped out of her worst nightmare.

I WISH HUMANITY

Ragini Kamendra Swati

Humanity isn't a race,

Although people are so busy in their pace.

Humanity is about to vanish.

Every soul is evil from inside.

No one is playing a fair game.

I wish humanity & longing for peace.

This world will be a beautiful place.

Just, we need to become a human being.

We human become so materialistic.

Evil rises like a poison in humanity.

Evil is stalking our mind & sanity.

So we need to unite against this immorality.

LAW OF SIN

Muskan Dhamgaye

The world is dangerous

Not because of the evils but also of the people who do nothing

for it

The biggest enemy of humans are humans itself

We can think but only of what suits us best

Creativity is beautiful but sometimes it's dangerous

We accused each other

Bread should be free

Shelter should be free

We must regain our sanity

Before we start killing one another

It is the multitudes madness

A vast collective madness

We can be good but we can't do well; deep in down we all have

a darkest heart.

Sometimes we quail, evil make us quail

There is different definition of evil.

LIFE MUST GO ON

Sonal Torane

We are breathing in this gloomy air!
I have realized this as the reality has
hit me hard!
Reality is "Exploitation has ruined
the lives of many!"
Reality is "Starvation has shattered the
lives of many!"
Reality is "Deadly diseases are spreading all over
the world!"
We all have become dead within as filthy depression has
spread all over the world!
It is making our life polluted and
our soul contaminated!
Why we live a life full of perturbations?
Where happiness is just a phase like our
dynamic seasons!
Where suffocation is the new trend
of being alive!
Where angels have more sins than demons!
Where purity is just a fake principle like a mirage
in the desert!
Great criminals are becoming great authorities rapidly!
Now, hypocrisy is in the blood of honesty!

Morality is in the hands of malignant innocents!
Humanity can never be associated with humans again!
As I breathe this filthy air, my life is turning
into living hell!
Oh dear, such vulnerability, I have to tolerate!
Getting on our knees, just for a moment of happiness and
satisfaction!
But as all these wicked things exist,
still life must go on!

THINGS HAVE CHANGED

s.a.ali

Nothing special.

Everything's same.

The moon comes and goes as usual

The sun rises as always.

But somewhere I feel

something has changed.

Is it me or is it the world?

I cannot understand.

I cannot differentiate.

More to the story, than what just appears.

Why is there so much

of chaos & bloodshed.

Why I see people in tears.

And I ask myself.

How could I be me?

How could I be free?

How could I ignore

the things that are happening.

How could I stop the worlds blackening?

The world that I knew.

is no more the same?

I don't know if you've noticed or not.

But things are changing.

And things have changed.

OH MY EVIL!
mohit chhabra

Oh my dear evil

I wonder why people scared from you,

I scared from them

Respecting cow & disrespecting their own mother who carried

them in their

womb for 9 months,

Throwing acid on a girl just because

she said no, or

Just killing each other for wealth,

Creating riots in the name of religion,

Judging people on the basis of their skin colour & so on

These humans are scarier than you & what kind of humanity is

this

I would love to be like you rather than these humans...

I CHOOSE TO BE...

Mohit Ananda

I choose to be free,

From rules and regulations,

From you and other relations,

The haunting thoughts of separations,

From all my doings and actions,

Let me fly high on the sky,

Set me free, tell me goodbye,

The chains of restrains are killing me,

The unbearable pains are stabbing me,

Your love is like a bed of rose,

Give it to the worthy,

and let me have what I chose.

IS LIFE WORTH LIVING?

Sakshi Sehrawat

"He is a gentleman" they say;
"He looks like a one" so says she.
He is a hunter and she is the prey;
Yes, this is his cruel reality.

He comes home late every night,
She keeps the food prepared.
But that doesn't fill his appetite,
So it's time for her to be scared.

Of course, she is his "beloved" wife,
Taken synonymous to private property
Imposing on her all his lies,
Revealing the evil behind his humanity.

He beats her as if she's not human,
Wishes to kill her or prove her insane.
In hope to marry another woman,
He ends up his wife diurnal in pain.

Felonious is what he does
And disgraceful is called the lady.
The society's decision I find bogus,
Petrified of the evils by humanity.

IS IT HUMANITY?

Haniya Azfar Fathima

Trees mourn for the dreadful loss,

Of their loved ones being chopped off

Oceans and seas snivel with grief,

For they are being dumped with debris.

Animals sob as their shelter gets embezzled,

As they have no means to dwell.

Birds weep as they apparently lose their lives

Just because of the technical radiation.

We cut their wings and steal their skins,

Despite knowing that they are filthy sins.

Distinction in the name of caste and creed,

Reveals nothing can satisfy the human greed.

Know that there is an outcome for every deed,

Can't you evade how much ever you plead?

Quenching the disgusting desires of mankind,

We all fail to realise we are the evils of humanity.

THE YIN AND YANG

Thahaseen M Hussain

Man- A cross breed individual of

Dominant beast and a recessive angel.

He belongs to the family of mosquitoes

Drinks blood of his own kith and kin.

He brutally kills people

And comes up with #save life

He prays for his good life

And also stalks his prey from other lives.

Insane man- Grow up!!

First drop of rain on a fully burnt hut

Or an ocean of water on a dead fish

Bring back no lives.

Stay raw and real.

HUMILIATION

Fatima Riaz

The wolf romped around

Silenced her every sound

Brutally, her dignity shed

Her soul tearfully bled

The Earth wreathed in pain

The sky whimpered, she was plundered in rain

Unaware of the beast, helpless were the trees

Defilement brought life to its knees

The clouds will always cry

The ocean of agony will never dry

When will such crimes be solved?

Pity to those angelic souls who get involved.

SELFISH WORLD

Jude Halleluyah

Amartya Sen's Poverty, evil and crime illustrates that poverty leads to crime. Even George Bernard Shaw argued that "the greatest of evil and worst of crimes is poverty". But the truth and the main cause of evil is the factor that is behind the poverty. The poverty is something which can be controlled. But now-a-days, in this world of capitalism, where they give importance to capitalist, so called big shots, owners and politicians. In this cruel world, where everyone tries to fill their own pocket. Instead of filling the pocket of people who work for them.

People had to live their own with the small amount of money. And when the need and demand increases in the family, their demands couldn't be acquired and were remained unsettled. Both the politicians who were chosen by the people in the name of democracy and the owners of company or factories. Greed, selfish, pride of an individual leads to hijacking the rights and prosperity of others which leads them to be in poverty which leads make a crime in order to fill their tummy. It is a thing which is beyond the hand of ordinary man. When the superiors are selfish and greedy filling their pockets and providing whatever their family wants instead of providing what they need.

They took away the prosperity which is destined for others. Only thing to control the poverty is to share everything with our fellow citizens in equal halves. We will share if we consider everyone as our brother and sister. We must be secular in thoughts or there must be no religion. When we are distinguished and classified which gives some kind of superiority over others and suppress others which help to take over them. They are intending to do crime. But no one in the world ever wants to sacrifice his comfort zone for a stranger, even for their relatives. It is a selfish world after all.

INTREPID SHE

Abigail Ocean

Insults hurled
Mind strong
Valliant I stand
Clothes torn.

Yes, I am she
That sex worker
Whom you detest
On the street
In that bar.

For years,
This trade has been on
Yes, trade
Of lust, pure lust

Bodies embossed, uniquely
Even soul sold
I still nod
For that money note.

Days come
Nights go by
Customers praise me
But they lack humanity

Nothing contends me
That note
That dripping praise
Mixed with malice

Got haughty,
Thought it was in my control
But no,
No one can conquer
The rough state of affairs.

When things get hard
Hard enough, to swallow the morsel
"All for my Kiara"
I assure myself.

UNHEARD CRIES

Karan Veer Bharadwaj

The whole is boring and nobody gives a damn.
Our nation is dying nobody can make
the riots calm.
This is it.
The future the leaders wished for.
Homophobia, Tran's phobia and Islam phobia everything is
going well, Humans are right? What are they?
Wars and bloodshed everywhere yet everyone
stay quiet.
Violence happens, but the spectators go blind.
This is the new era the people wished for?
This is what we get as a gift of New Year?
The only thing that's new is the types of fear.
Slowly, hatred is winning and love and
peace is dying.
Nobody can hear how loud Earth is crying.
The battle over powers is yet not over.
The fear in mind and hearts are still not over.
Every moment my body does shiver.
Every second increases the intensity of fear.
The new future is here,
Oh! I mean the new fear.

I'm out of words to express,
I surely lack of awareness,
But I know that life now is nothing less than hanging on a
broken harness.
This is the new world everyone wished for,
Now end is knocking on the door,
Now nothing more I got to say,
Battles I can't fight anymore,
Just going to wait till my end is here.

ENCOMPASS BY HIS MONSTERS

Sonali Baral

He created a list of his monsters
I saw the cuts on his hand
Of everyone who broke his come
And burn his precious promised land.

He created a list of his monsters
I wanted him to forget them all
Between his monsters and himself
I decided to create a wall.

He created a list of his monsters
There was something missing in between
I was so lost in trying to fix him
I didn't see where I fitted in.

He created a list of his monsters
I helped him forget all of them
I wondered why he forgot me
Then I realized I was one of them.

A WORLD OF SINNERS

Priyanshi Mussadi

Sinners all around,

Soul is black everywhere

There was a time it was red,

Full of love and care

But now, it's rare

For all are busy

Being sinners you see!

Who are sinners?

What do they do?

Sinners do sin

Hahaha,

In short,

They commit wrong actions

For which they don't repent!

But, the question is,

Should they repent?

Should they penance?

After all why would the world correct?

Are they not smart enough to repent?

After all, for long we have been taught,

"The one who does, it the one who bears."

"Therefore, a person who sins can be everything but not a pure

soul."

HUMANITY BECOMES EVIL

M.Shanmuga Priya

Humanity is like painting,

Filled with all colours and shades.

Humanity is like bleeding heart,

Cut with many sharp blades.

Humanity is like never ending story,

That always begins with behaviour.

Humanity is like space everlasting,

That fills bitterness with bliss.

Humanity is like circle of eternity,

Always there to take for free.

Humanity is like open clear pool,

Where no hate can dare swim.

Humanity is captured sunset,

Where the warmth never grows dim.

Humanity always loves gold,

And they are selfish to become bold.

So, Humanity becomes Evil.

ONE MORE...

Mahammad Rizwan Ahamed

Have you ever experienced a pellet rain on ramshackle? Have you felt being sucked by mire filled with plight? I felt that on 14/5/1997.

I am.....No, I won't tell my name because there are more judgmental on this land than the droplets in the ocean. I was from an impoverished family and a wicked society. I was brought up by my father. My mother left us very early, maybe she didn't want to be an extra burden for the family. So, my father worked relentlessly. I was battered with words by some sick people. But I had a bloom in all this gloom, my sister who was 5 years younger to me.

She was very supportive, generous, funny and a bit annoying as well. We were going to school which was odd at those days in those places. My sister was fascinated with the new phase of her life. She was curious in exploring facts. She had a hard time in school. But she neither bothered nor complained about those issues because these issues were never above her determination to study. My father was having a tough time at work. So I quit my studies to help my father at work and my sister at studies. We were having a contended life.

But one day, I was affected with chicken pox. I was lying on the bed for around 10 days. But my health did not improve. So my father and my sister were worried. Then my sister was said a myth that I had committed a sin for which I was being punished and a girl from the house has to go wearing a white dress, jasmines and coconut for deity and please the goddess on the hill this midnight alone to save me. 13/5/1997 (10.48 PM)

My beloved innocent sister went secretly as my father would never let her go. She went there but couldn't return. She became a scapegoat in the hands of cold-blooded people. Those who treated us as Untouchables......raped my sister ruthlessly by choking cloth in her mouth. They also scratched, beat, pricked, hit her with coconut like psychopaths and burnt her finally. She was in an age that she couldn't even express her brutal experience.

Next day, I recovered and went to the spot, the sight was horrible to watch and terrible to breath. White dress had turned to red with blood stains. Jasmines fragrance faded against the corpse smell. My father wept at the sight and bit the dust there itself. I did the funeral for both of them. The case was closed by bribing. Then my sister was called....Hooker. Our village was so far that my chaos left unheard.

In this solely battle I had two options: One was to kill assailants myself; the second was to just move on like nothing ever happened....

But I chose the 3rd way. I put my blood and sweat for my vengeance. 16 years later, I became a lawyer. I argued our case and won it. Then I wished my father and sister

"Rest in peace".

It was not the end. I argued 454 unjustified cases till now and won.

Today this count will be "1 more"....

BURNING PIECES

Shangamitra Chakraborty

Unveiling the channel to paradise today,

Letting out the hidden desires enclosed between entangled

columns,

Concealed, those yearns and emotions,

Setting them unconfined, untamed,

leisurely night...

Setting barriers apart today, new limits await,

Tides within, entangled to the rhythm of beats, begging for

more...

Fix your gaze on my valley, undressing

emotions beneath,

Pour me into the waves of your moistness, warming veiled

urges gingerly.

Tongue escalading the unmasked beats, leaving marks of

ecstasy,

Shivers down the spine...

Lips brushing against the undiscovered land, sipping holy

emanations down the quim...

Push me closer, closer to the

maddening essence,

Unbind the monster encaged...

Thrusting the unspoken shots of desire, charge me up with

your fire...

Digging out the path to pleasure,

Naked soul moaning with desire.

A SMEARED ROSE

Jyoti Gogia

She was basking in the avalanche of applauds.
Her beautiful pieces of art were complemented.
Replenished with such immense pleasure,
She forgot to look at the time by her watch.
"Damn it's ten already", she had jitters.
She felt a tinge of sharp intuition,
All at once swallowing her smile,
She picked her bag and ran towards aisle.
Wishing for wings to reach home on time
But ah! All efforts were in vain,
Her man was already caught up at home.
A doctor well known for his velvety voice
Lacing fringes of spears in his tone,
"Could you not see the time?" he hissed on her
And then started a round of torture,
His belt had peeled her skin on the back.
Crying and moaning was her daily routine.
Permission she needs for every single breath.
As she was told that she was a woman.
Her existence depends on the pity of a man.

IMITATIONS OF PEN

M Dhivya

The world is dried

With a melancholic heart we live;

Sealed from the festivities all around

With a crippled heart, life goes on.

Many wish for death

Others fear death itself;

Some run behind money others

barely have any

Life is a theory yet to be accepted.

We are the imitation of the pen

Creators of our own work

Most filled with joy and unbearable pain

The poets are the poem itself indefinable

As it resonates and conveys

I will write no more...

Cause there is so much to say.

UNDERNEATH

Sayantan Das

How can I behave?
For I can finally breathe the fire from
your skin.
For I have longed to love you
with stony fingers.
For the nature's lost treasure stuck in time
Snacked in rose lit valise
Shamelessly inviting me
To run riot in them
How can I behave?
Could I behave?
When your temples touched mine
While you rode up to the sky
Like Icarus wanting to get burnt and shine
In need of air and desires divine
Could I behave?
Should I still behave?
When your soul met mine
Finding solace combine
When it feels so divine
Whilst praying in your shrine
An exchange of elixirs
Should I still behave?

A PERFECT WIFE: A TALE OF DOMESTIC VIOLENCE

Deepali Gandhi

A lot of sleepless nights
After every scream and fight
It was she to run into your arms
Know no better way to make you calm.

So many disappointments and let downs
Every night in bed this queen lost her crown
Still in the morning first to wake
Shattered pieces she gather and take.

Whole day she walks around with a smile
Life for her has never been facile
You enjoy parties she waits for dinner
Each passing day she is getting thinner.

Still she never leaves your side
By your rule book she always abide
Simply beautifying your life
She is an epitome of a perfect wife.

UNTOLD EMOTIONS OF A DESTITUTE MOTHER

Mandavi Verma

Most of People say that we feel the pain only when

we get hurt.

But, there are some pains that occur

without injury.

What's the real pain?

A helpless mother who couldn't save her child even while

keeping her alive in her belly.

Even after alive her child, she couldn't even see

her child.

She couldn't take out her child in world.

What could be more painful for her than this?

The reason of that mother's

Voiceless death is only and human.

Human haven't only committed the crime of killing wildlife but

have too killed

an Innocent mother.

They killed an innocent child too

They have given true evidence of their humanity by taking the

life of an innocent animal.

Can humans really be so cruel?

Yes they're.

They became so cruel that they didn't take pity on an innocent
animal.
If they can't feed animals,
They have no right to poison them.
Human not only so cruel but also indictable!
That's why they took their vengeance
with helplessness.

What was her fault?
She believed in human
But it was her illusion.
Those humans too are clean hearted like her.
Human killed her faith badly.
She eventually proved to be wrong.
Human betrayed her.
She was completely defeated.
Finally he had to die.
Even God did not have mercy on her!
God created nature for all
Animals too have an equal right to live here.
Like humans, they too have feelings.
They understand us even after being helpless.
So why don't we as humans understand them?
Humans have no right to persecute them.
Human has committed a scandalous crime by killing a helpless
mother.

Human killed the hopes of a voiceless.

They're worse than animals.

They're wilder than animals.

God must be ashamed of to create human.

It wouldn't be wrong to say that humanity

is no more.

May the soul of hopeless mother rest in peace.

THE ROAD OD EVIL

Suman Meena

Evil, a Deadliest Poison

Denotes Absence of Good

Evil Influence is Like a Glue

Once Sticks to Your Soul

Destroys Your All Goodness

& one can do no Good thereafter.

It Incurs Feeling of Hatred

Lead the Path towards Darkness

It Gives a Mischievous Satisfaction

By Throwing off Rails of Other People's Goals

To Unstable their Life

Gives Joy of Seeing Another Person in Pain.

One Must Recognize Evil Elements

Of their Internal World

& Start Working Untiringly

On eradicating them.

CRYSTAL GLOBE OF SMOG
Vanshita Tuli

I turned away and closed my heart

Shrugged my feelings and i lost

Promise to never love.

Love that is mere allure

It's difficult to blind eyes,

despite they witness ravishing sites

difficult to teach your soul.

Soul that died last time

Someone who completes the puzzle

Puzzle of your kind

Heart fears again

Am i travelling again back in time?

Trust is false and faiths like smog

There was a time I told you

About all that ached inside

Things i held so sacred deep inside my globe

New being start to travel and flow down bars

What is she like?

I was told like melancholy of flowers

It's hard to fall in love with someone

When they see mixed parts of your soul

When they understand darkest and dustiest corners

of your mind

But these fears like light

Instigates the impulse of realise

Evokes the volcano of past

And reminds me not to repeat the mistake

like last time.

NEED A QUICK ATTENTION

Monika Dimnikar

Not just a phrase

Not just topic

Not just a social issue

It's a nature

It's existing in our society deeply in

different faces

I saw an Instagram story few days back

A 9 month old girl was raped in India

A 43 year old mentally Challenged woman was

raped in Mumbai.

Two people who even don't know that they

are being abused..

If this is not an evil action then what is it???

Is it a thing which should be ignored??

Obviously no...

This is one of the biggest evil actions seen in our society... Why

rapes happen? Why people become so cruel???

Is it because of that person who raped? Or because of that

person who is accused...

Answer is it's because of the thinking, nature and way of
looking at different things of that person
who did evil action..
Sometimes people go to such extent where the only way they
have to kill some individual to get rid of problem or to take
revenge...
No one is born with an evil natured mind-set... It's the
surrounding who creates or who feeds these kinds of thoughts
to individuals...
I think we should take small steps to remove all the bad vibes
from our surrounding...
Not by fighting but by making people's mind-set heading
towards beautiful thoughts of education, progress, happiness..
Rather to divert them towards revenge, murder, rapes etc...
We can change the whole scenario just by finding out ways to
communicate...

Shhh! DON'T RAISE YOUR VOICE!

Anjali Srivastava

Shhh! don't raise your voice up! They often cajole her, "don't
raise your voice up, your throat will get choked."
"He is bit short-tempered, if he ever throws the plate
full of food,
Then just wrap yourself with
a sheet of patience,
And pick up the plate silently.
The thing is sometimes he gets angry."
"He is bit short-tempered,
If he ever raises hands on you,
Then just give shelter your scars
under your veil.
The thing is sometimes he gets angry."
"He is bit short-tempered,
If he ever gazes you to stop talking,
Then just close your mouth with a lock of silence and put the
keys in his pocket.
The thing is sometimes he gets angry."
And there they got success!
She is not speaking anything.
They say may be her throat is choked.

WAS IT A FAULT?

Divya Anandan

Was it a fault?
To anticipate a halt
In the self-run of humans.
Was it a fault?
To anticipate a fair sense,
When humans were fabricated with
higher sense.
Was it a fault?
To anticipate a love back
When humans were implied for a love track.
Was it a fault?
To anticipate a learn,
Learning to swim in the middle of the ocean,
Knowing its deep, knowing I can't, still a want,
Knowing I can't discover people,
People who are selfless,
In this exclusive era of self.
But still, this heart drenches in needs,
So I am a human indeed,
A mere human being trapped,
And constrained with desires,
Who desires humanity?

Was it a fault?
To anticipate humanity.
In the human.

THE WEIGHT ISSUE
Rupali Gore

Vanmala, a school topper, had joined the first year of junior college. With an intellectual excellence, a cheerful, amicable personality, a beautiful visage, she was a favourite friend of many and teachers also knew her, by her name.

There was an Elocution competition, in college. Vanmala participated. D-Day dawned. Donning a dashing black pleated skirt and a white shirt, Vanmala was confidence personified. The judge was a famous author. The competition began. It was Vanmala's turn to speak, her opportunity to release her feelings, before an audience.

She rose to the occasion! Vanmala stood in front of the loudspeaker and the audience. Vanmala spoke," Hello, Today's topic is ' Society's evil '. I was a thin child, with no chubby cheeks. All the aunties, grandmothers and friends used to tease me for being a ' thin stick '. They had a dietary advice to give to my mother. Ironically, this thin girl was good at sports and studies, much better than their daughters and granddaughters! This ' stick ' girl was blessed with an enviable stamina, thanks to healthy food made by her mother, her loving parents and God's grace! After the mid nineties' success of India's slim models, in international beauty pageants, societal parameters of beauty changed from ' well-built women ' to tall, slim women '. As a teenager, I gained weight during this period. So I was labelled a ' big, fat hen ', ' gunny bag ' and many such abusive adjectives were used. Why should I be labelled and written off for my weight? Who sets these standards? Is having a standardized, perfect weight an assurance of a healthy body and a healthy mind? The answer is a ' NO! '. Why should I be bogged down by these standards? Why should these judgemental persons judge and mock others? Don't they have any other meaningful work to do? In our country, Ganesha - lord of beginnings is worshipped. He is bestowed with a great intellect.

Courage and a well-built body. So, why is a person, taunted for his weight...? Why can't a person be respected and allotted space for him? My speech is more of a series of questions, which the society, needs to answer ... If every person channelizes his energies in a constructive work and encourages others, life will be a better place to breathe in. Look at the world of vegetables, there is a space for a huge pumpkin as well as for the svelte French beans!

Such teasing and mockery can shatter a person, emotionally. He can suffer from a low self-esteem, low self-worth and a low confidence level.

Verbal abuse is a harmful Social evil, which needs to be checked. Don't hear the verbal abuse silently, reply assertively. That is possible at an individual and at a collective level. It will be successful, if everyone is united!

Thank you! "

Result – standing ovation, third prize and Dean displayed her speech on the notice board. Vanmala was delighted!

CURSED BEAUTY

Shikha shivangee

Trying to look into the mirror, a small little girl stands on her
tiptoes

Loosely draping her mother's saree, otiose tries to disguise like
her beneath a long veil

Filthily polishing her tiny lips with red lipstick, and her fingers
colored with the rest of it

Managing the almost falling off oversized bangles like a
veteran, while grasping her sweeping 'pallu'

A resembling face scolds with a hint of conceding laughter, to
come to sleep soon

Two decades later, trying to look into the mirror, a young lady
barely stands
on her stilettos

Sumptuously draping her saree over a glittery bodice
divulging her bosom

Elegantly coloring the lips, conceding the darkened, bitten
lower flap

Managing the almost bleeding off wrist like a veteran, while
wearing the Lilliputian bangles

A familiar voice scolds, with a hint of voyeuristic glee, to come
to bed soon...

ROOT OF EVIL

K.N.Namratha Ram

World is a dangerous place,
Ultimately sunken in solace,
But a lot of people are fake,
It's not for anyone's sake,
Not a chance of intentions to be pure,
There's always a root of evil.

No one's born evil but with spirits enslaved,
They get hurt and harm others when outraged,
Craving the power to rule over good,
Humans are creatures easily misunderstood,
The good only appears to be temporary,
There's always a root of evil.

Judging what they perceive,
Evil spirited always deceive,
They always serve their ego,
Their good nature is just a placebo,
Sometimes, man wants what's forbidden,
There's always a root of evil.

SUSPICIOUS HUMANITY: THE ENDLESS THREAD

Rabia Banu

Let us explore the difference between evil
and scary;
People are so immersed in their glory;
There comes a year 2020;
People came to know their insane reality;

Increasing demand in the price of their life;
Has to fulfil it to prevent afterlife;
Nothing changes every day,
People are all reborn with vain in a way.

When they are tired eventually;
Blaming others without
wisdom unconditionally;
Flashes keep flickering at the sites of calamity;
Forget their help in their site, full of insanity.

Need to remind the spelling of MERCY;
To stop bullying the weak to become sturdy
Drowning in the waves of evil inside;
But posing like a pro with a evil sticker
like a Bride.

WITHOUT ANY SHAME!

Shwetha.A.S

She dreamt of a bright future,
Along with the dream man of her life.
Little did she know it was not his true nature?
That's so fake, hidden deep just to avoid strife.
Good things take time and his face did reveal,
Breaking her into millennial pieces like shreds.
Has she really lost her life's zeal?
Not realizing a thing, she has lost
her last thread.
Her parents no more, as they were
asked to pay dowry,
Without any kind of benevolence, the groom's side
did pester.
Could have given some time to pay
without causing worry,
They were so blinded with their evil
yet fake gestures.
Good health is so very important to earn and
make a living,
Not like asking dowry without any shame for
your surviving!

THE NIGHT OF HALLOWEEN
Ranjana Chakraborty

It was a dark and gloomy Saturday night. The party venue was the old abandoned hospital nearby Graveyard. Loud music and people were dancing in their spooky costumes. While we shared our laughter, we decided to roam around the venue. We came outside from the room and the hallway was empty, it felt like we came to different environment.

We heard noises from upstairs so decided to go there. We saw nurses and doctors busily at their stations attending to their obligations. At first we thought they must running their business illegally. So we tried to ask one nurse about the things. We called her, but she didn't responds. While moving towards her, she crossed from our body like a soul. We got scared and thought to leave that place.

While coming to downstairs, we saw the dark green curtain of the emergency room rises to gust of the wind and reveal two bodies. One with breaking neck seemed to be an athlete and another one was armed force. After moving ahead we felt someone was behind us. I decided not to look back and move further. Later we heard a crying, one my friend turned back and he mentioned the little girl is white frock was seeking of help. He decided to help her. I told him it was a trap, but he didn't

listen and went.

After a minute or two we heard his crying, we looked back. There were more along with that little girl and was dragging him through the hallway and scratched his body. They killed him through the hammer. We all were getting scared and thought to run away and decided to go to party. Both these men were alive just a few minutes ago when they were brought in, but now they were lifeless with eyes open as if they were trying to fend off an invisible force to prevent it from taking their souls.

They were stabbed through scissors by the two shadows, still they tried to runaway .While crossing the hallway we saw blankets and equipment's were scattered with bloodied all around was lying on the floor. Later we saw a shadow that's as black as night and whose face was hidden by a hood and he carried scythe. He was still chasing us.

While running another friend of mine fell from stairs and hit his head towards wall. I asked him to get up and leave that place with me. The shadow came nearer to us and holding the scythe. We screamed and fear gripped all over us. Suddenly, the demonic force split us far away from each other.

I was thrown out of the window, everything flickered. Then the door slammed shut, and after a gust of wind, an evil laughed slowly vanish into thin air and everything went silent and after that I went black.

When I woke up I found myself alive but in grief as I lost my close friends.

EVIL DEVIL

Zia

Looking at ourselves in the mirror
We'll find two different personalities
One is as beautiful as spring
Other is terrible like calamities.

No one can estimate about
What are we in next moment?
Somewhere corrupt and menacing
Somewhere a daring foeman.

Acting ruthless to fulfil
All that we need,
Not considering needy and poor
Who come to us and plead.

Today one who was supposed?
To be generous and kind
Unfortunately he is the most
Self-centred and blind.

HELLO EVIL!

Ms Divya Dilip Shetty

Evils by humanity is such that we are
destroying ourselves,
Our brain is heading towards technology,
Our mind is getting rust with negativity,
Our heart is pressurized & pumping slowly,
Our body is getting weaker day by day
Our soul is weeping with pain,
Our hands are continuously operating gadgets,
Our legs are tired of climbing the stairs,
Our eyes are seeking success,
Our mouth has forgotten to communicate,
Our ears are waiting for answers,
Our life is like an imprisonment nowadays,
We have forgotten to cherish,
Together with the nature & its creatures,
We have forgotten to live,
As time passes by,
We have forgotten to laugh,
It feels as if we are cursed,
Don't we need to heal?
& start living life once again?

AFTER ALL...

Amritha Varshini R

Her angelic smile, twinkling eyes
Whispered million dreams.
Innocence of seven year old lass
Trusted him, the next-door monster
When his poison honeyed words plunged,
As magnetic care and love, little gem,
Overjoyed but oblivious, ambled.
He wangled her to a deserted place
To persuade his brutal pleasure!
Thenceforth stabbing her brutally
On her little face, tender neck!
Eternal rest embraced her, his favour!
Endowing utmost brutal pain,
Well pleased his ruthless pleasure.
Later, cold body deserted in a bush,
Half naked with fragments of cloths,
Magnificent food for ant and fly.
Humanity perished, in fact slaughtered,
When his pleasure stabbed her tender body!
After all.... She was just seven!

THE WEEPING WILLOW THAT WEPT
Mobani Biswas

My feet crunched the forest floor; a chill penetrated down my spine. Swivelling a torch I gauged my surrounding. One thought was constantly echoing in my mind- "How did I land up in this forest?"

Suddenly I heard a wail and cautiously inched closer to the sound. I came to a standstill when I saw a majestic tree glistening in the moonlight, drops of water falling from its branches and leaves. I don't know what possessed me, but I reached out to touch it and the leaves rustled in response. The wailing swiftly ceased; I looked around, noticing my moves been watched by the

trees surrounding me. The tree then thundered- "I see you have arrived human!" I asked- "Who are you? Why were you waiting for me and why were you weeping? In my world, do you know trees cannot speak?"

The tree replied-"O yes, I am the Willow tree, guide of this forest. In your world, people refer to me as the Weeping Willow. Humans give various reasons as to why they think I weep but today I'll tell you the actual reason behind it."

Stumped that I was watching a tree talk, I simply nodded for the Willow tree to carry on with its monologue. It continued, "Before the advent of the 20th century, science did not even acknowledge our vitality. Then a human named Jagadish Chandra Bose proved we too feel pain and shed tears, we get sad and we also fear but the only issue is that we can't speak. But even in the 21st century, we are still bearing the atrocities of humans. I heard that humans have laws; they imprison or hang the person charged with murder. Tell me human, do you charge anyone for the murder

of a tree?"

I wanted to stand up for the human race but how could I? Deep down I knew we have wronged them all along.

The willow tree rambled on, "Every drop of tear I shed is for each of my friends and family members killed. I wait with bated breath for the day those humans come for me and hack at my barks. Humans write their will before they die, hence I called you here to bear witness to my wounds and to inform your world about

why I cry."

Tears trickled down my face and I closed my eyes; abruptly I felt a jerk and on reopening my eyes I came face to face with an article on my computer screen which read "Why Does a Weeping Willow Tree Weep?"

Bewildered I move my head to see my mother pinning me down with her questioning look.

I excitedly got up from the seat and said, "Mom, I know exactly why the weeping willow weeps!"

My mother nodded bemusedly and said- "I know too, when the raindrops fall from its branches, it looks like the tree is weeping."

She turns to go and all I can say is- "No mom, that's not the case!"

GIVE HER WINGS TO FLY

Konki Kamal Sharon

In life full of dramatic versions her

story roared

But no one has dare to lend her a hand

She always remained as the victim of snored

Do ever know of making something life

that too end.

It's not we call life; it makes a woman

to go through evil

After all her ambitions are unnoticed

and unheard

Stepping her feet out of the house humanity turned

into devil

Nor this society gives her the hand her story

gone unheard.

She was a little baby but born as a girl with

overloaded cuteness

Which made a man to cover his eyes with lust just

on a small kid?

Do the societies where a baby has come give her

hope to survive

No, evil humanity of lust always stood like a lid.

She is a mother, daughter, sister yet she is alone

Survival of her was questioned by society

Not for her achievements they stood her by her side but they

left all alone

Born as a girl makes a future generation but evil humanity

will not make her survive.

If a girl can walk on the ambitions, there the day of support

flourishes

Give her the wings of courage and hope

Let her fly with the dreams, be like a brother and stand like a

father

Little the favour she needs from the society.

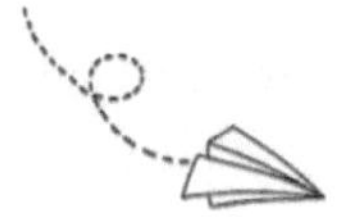

THE YAZIDIAN GENOCIDE

Dikshita Sarma

'*LET ME GO!*'......

Thousands of Women screaming together

Their terrifying pleads echoed the area

As they were being pulled away

By Hordes of Bearded Men

With the look of Iconic Demon

Their Sights of Ravish, scanning through the

bodies of Females

Lips drooling with lust,

Eyes filled with anger and Disgust

That even the God of Evil would be put to shame.

Once the golden deserts of Syria

Turned in a flash into a dumping area

Filled with corpses

Spilled with Rivers of Blood everywhere

Men and Children beheaded mercilessly before the eyes

Women pulled away like animals

And being abducted in masses......

That's the last thing she could remember

Before she was being forced away too

By the Pretenders as Humans

And her Life being forced into a horrifying Mess.......

FADING OF HUMANITY

Ujjwal Shree

Good will never make you kneel,

Evil is something you don't feel.

Greed is the seed of

All evil deeds,

Killing of female foeticide, what has happened

to mankind...?

Has mankind and society forgotten humanity,

Or have they accepted cruelty.

To the society dowry system is a big curse,

Evils like human trafficking are making the situation more

badly.

Where's our humanity,

When we need it the most,

Or is it just imagination,

A figment of a

Ghost?

HIPOCRISY EXPOSED

Jude Fernandes

Preaching morals
Of loving my enemy,
While bitterly hating
Thy own neighbour...

Advocating for lives
Of simple pleasure,
While secretly stashing
Piles of treasure...

Stabbing daggers into
Anguished mankind,
While washing off guilt,
No claimed fault to find...

Painting rainbow spectrums
That glows and sparks,
While you reject the light
And embrace the dark...

Hope overshadowed
By doom of profanity,
Will I be silenced for exposing?
The evil of humanity?

EVILS ALL AROUND

Chaitrali Umesh Baheti

Tears of destruction are drizzling with rain,
The nature we once cherished is crying in pain.
Caged in society, we all are trying to break through
that chain.
Sometime belittled by someone or sometime just treated with
disdain.
Differences we all have, of religions
and opinions,
But we forget that we're still trapped in same bodies with
emotions.
Raped by humanity and trapped by relations,
United by universe yet divided by nations.
Everyone's selfish hiding their motives
behind mask.
Who to trust is really a difficult task.
Disturbed with ourselves, questions
we often ask.
While some are just boasting their ego
with fake bask.
So what is wrong or what is right,
The havocs within us are just living in plight.
Some raise voices, some use inks to write.

With others or themselves, we all just fight.
Justice we all are demanding.
Still waiting for dawns of happy ending.
But at last the evils keep raising and rising,
Making the holy angels turn into ashes with
continuous burning.

HUMANITY VS RESPONSIBILITY

Dhanya Ravi

A girl went to a famous place well known for preaching human values and spreading humanity. After visiting all the places around, she entered a shop inside the same compound. The shop sells that place's own manufactured products ranging from fabrics, brass vessels to cloth bags etc.

The girl walked around the shop to check out the objects to buy something as a memory of her visit to that place. She was not satisfied with any of the products, so she decided not to buy anything from there. At that moment she never knew that she will have an unforgettable experience there for the memory. When she was almost to leave the shop, she noticed a rope bag hanging on the hook of a swing like set up. The swing was made up of a heavy wooden slab tied with ropes to the roof, with hooks from the slab the rope bags were hanging.

The girl decided to check out the bag's quality, so she could purchase that. She went closer to the rope bag and took the bag from the hook with no force but gently using her right hand. All of a sudden, the swing rope loosened and the wooden slab from the swing fell down on her left hand. But trying to save the objects on the swing from falling she kept holding the heavy wooden slab, in order to avoid a collapse.

She expected someone around there will help her out, by getting the slab from her seeing her suffering from pain. Though paining she continued to hold the heavy slab with hope of getting a help as she believed in humanity. But she got a heart break seeing the upcoming actions.

A few people present in the shop, came near that girl when the others were busy with their own works and left it unnoticed. There came two lady staffs of the shop rushing in the girl's direction. She felt happy and relaxed seeing them, but then little did she know that those ladies have no humanity. Those ladies cared only for the shop products, she thought may be that was their responsibility.

The girl's hope for humanity started to fade away, and for one last time she cried out loud for help "could anyone help me??? Please get this slab from me, it's hurting!!!". Then came two boys near the girl, they were the customers at the shop. She got relief that someone finally came to her rescue, but then for her disappointment, the boys were helping those staffs to safe guard the products only.

After all this happened within few minutes, after setting all the shop products the one lady staff came near the girl. That staff pulled the rope bag from the girl's right hand with a rude look. And finally, now all these great people with no humanity got the slab from the girl. The girl felt pain instead of relief, not for her injury but for the human's rude behaviour.

She walked to the door with a heavy heart, but stopped at once, looked back at those people in the shop and said - "Are you people really humans??? You value lifeless objects over human pain and emotions?? Looking at those staffs she said - Shame on you! You might value your responsibility, but not at the cost of humanity. She travelled back home with so many unanswered questions in her mind.

"What if a kid or an elderly person was in my situation? Will those staffs behave differently, if I was a customer who had a big purchase in their shop? Was there any mistake from my side? So, humanity vs responsibility, which is more important? She never got an answer so far.

START FROM INDIVIDUALS

Subhendu Kumar Dash

Vile and immoral acts,
Often characterized by,
Their detrimental effects
On social health are often
Considered as heinous.
But are self-injurious;
As people of society
Create those and get suffered,
By those too.
One creates and then,
The rest follow him,
Without even realizing
Its effect on the society.
We often see our profit and
Do such activities which,
Lead to devastating effects.
We can't stop these unless,
One thinks deeply about it,
And then changes himself.
It should be started
At an individual level.
Then only the evil can be eradicated.

People often take a stand against these but when it comes to
them then they just keep mum.
That's the real problem of our society.

MOTHER EARTH'S LETTER

Anagha Palathoor

Sombre mood sticks around

Cremation of Me

Is a teabag in hot water?

Emotions start leaking Essence too...

Seeking letters from heart

Soft by divine love

Never like before

I am almost barren.

Carcinogenic fumes around

My clotted wounds leaks

Why me?

Only quenched their thirst

But now evil of mortals

Make choking, holistic world.

A BUON INTENDITOR, POCHE PAROLE

(A word to the wise)

Save thee, save mother Earth.

THE ODD REALITY
Samriddhi Gupta

Where the world is going?

Feeling their warmth and enjoying.

But wait not everyone is same,

Some are evils in the shadow of human being.

Doing their criminal work,

Under the cover of beautiful jerk,

It will hurt by their playful game,

You will be surprised by the changeable fame

This is only every day's site,

Something will be new to you,

Something will be ripe,

And you have to be careful in dangerous unite.

SOMEONE LIKE YOU

Suman Kumar

I used to dream of someone like you,

To hold me tight and see me through,

To love my eyes and love my smile,

And when I'm scared stay with me a while,

But now I've got you I don't know what to do,

It's amazing this feeling I have for you,

When I look at you my heart melts to the floor,

Every day I love you more and more,

When life gets me down your always there,

A good heart like yours is very rare,

You're my world you're my universe my star,

I would never change a thing that you are,

All my worries and problems disappear,

When you hold me in your arms I have no fear,

The only fear I have that's true,

Is living my life without someone like you.